Fiona Finkelstein Meets Her Match !!

Aladdin

• • • • • New York London Toronto Sydney • • • •

Fiona Finkelstein Meets Her Match!!

Shawn K. Stout

Illustrated by Angela Martini

This book is a work of fiction. Any references to historical events, real people, or real locales are used
fictitiously. Other names, characters, places, and incidents are the product of the author's imagination, and
any resemblance to actual events or locales or persons, living or dead, is entirely coincidental.

ALADDIN
An imprint of Simon & Schuster Children's Publishing Division
1230 Avenue of the Americas, New York, NY 10020
First Aladdin paperback edition October 2010
Text copyright © 2010 by Shawn K. Stout
Illustrations copyright © 2010 by Angela Martini
All rights reserved, including the right of reproduction in whole or in part in any form.
ALADDIN is a trademark of Simon & Schuster, Inc., and related logo is
a registered trademark of Simon & Schuster, Inc.
Also available in an Aladdin hardcover edition.
For information about special discounts for bulk purchases, please contact Simon & Schuster
Special Sales at 1-866-506-1949 or business@simonandschuster.com.
The Simon & Schuster Speakers Bureau can bring authors to your live event. For more information
or to book an event contact the Simon & Schuster Speakers Bureau at 1-866-248-3049
or visit our website at www.simonspeakers.com.
Designed by Karin Paprocki
The text of this book was set in Perpetua.
Manufactured in the United States of America 0810 OFF
2 4 6 8 10 9 7 5 3 1
Library of Congress Cataloging-in-Publication Data
Stout, Shawn K.
Fiona Finkelstein meets her match!! / by Shawn K. Stout ;
illustrated by Angela Martini. — 1st Aladdin hardcover ed.
p. cm.
Summary: Fiona Finkelstein does not get along with Milo, a new student
in her Ordinary, Maryland, fourth-grade class, especially when he starts a meteorology club.
She responds by trying to start a matchmaking club.
ISBN 978-1-4169-7928-9 (hc)
[1. Schools—Fiction. 2. Clubs—Fiction. 3. Competition (Psychology)—Fiction. 4. Family life—
Maryland—Fiction. 5. Maryland—Fiction.] I. Martini, Angela, ill. II. Title.
PZ7.S88838Fk 2010 / [Fic]—dc22 / 2010026829
ISBN 978-1-4169-7110-8 (pbk) / ISBN 978-1-4424-0953-8 (eBook)

For Andy, my match

• Chapter 1 •

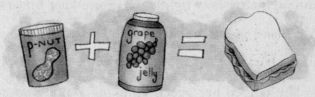

Fiona Finkelstein had a bad feeling.

It was the kind of feeling she got when she just knew that Mrs. Miltenberger packed a corned beef sandwich in her lunchbox, even though she's told her a gazillion times that she HATES corned beef more than she HATES anything else. Especially after learning that there was actually no corn in it. If there was one thing Fiona flat-out could not stand, it was food that lies.

Fiona didn't know exactly why she was having this feeling today. Maybe because today was the day Mr. Bland, her fourth-grade teacher, was going to draw names for new classroom jobs. For months, Fiona wanted to be picked for electrician. But no matter how tightly she crossed her fingers, Mr. Bland always pulled somebody else's name out of the bucket.

She tapped her green Thinking Pencil on her desk and looked at her best friend, Cleo Button, and Harold Chutney next to her. "I've decided if I don't get to be electrician this time, I'm going to stop taking baths."

"What will that do?" asked Cleo.

"I'll have so much stink on me that Mr. Bland will have to give me the job next time," said Fiona. "I'll tell him that he'll be smelling my stink until he pulls my name out of that bucket."

"Good idea," said Cleo, cracking her knuckles. "I hope I get to be line leader."

Harold pulled his finger out of his nose. "I want to be gardener."

"Gardener?" said Fiona and Cleo at the same time.

"Oh, Boise Idaho. What?" said Harold.

"That's the worst job there is," said Fiona. "There's only one plant that you get to water, and it's a cactus."

Harold shrugged. "What's so great about being electrician?"

Fiona shook her head. "It's only the best job ever. You get to plug in the TV and overhead projector. And work the DVD player."

"And turn off the lights," said Cleo, who was electrician the time before last.

"So?" said Harold, wiping his finger under his desk.

Fiona sighed. Besides being a nose-picker, Harold was the only kid she knew who said things like "Oh, Boise Idaho" and who didn't like cool things like plugs. Sometimes Fiona thought about the possibility that Harold was really an old lady disguised in a boy suit.

The bell rang just then. "Everybody quiet down," said Mr. Bland. "Before we get started, Principal Sterling is here with an important announcement."

"Good morning, everyone," said Principal Sterling. Her high heels clicked as she walked to the front of the classroom. A boy trailed close behind. He was tall and had spiky hair that made him even taller. "I'd like to introduce a new student who is joining your class." She put her hand on the boy's shoulder. "This is Milo Bridgewater, and he's just moved here to Maryland all the way from Minnesota."

The new boy, Milo, stuffed his hands into his pockets and looked down at his feet. Fiona was trying to remember where Minnesota was because there were lots of M-states and she got them all mixed up. It occurred to her then that Milo also starts with *M* and wasn't that funny. Fiona wondered why there weren't any states that started with *F* and

wasn't that unfair. And then she thought of one. "Florida!" she shouted in excitement.

Everyone looked at her. And then they cracked up. Except for Mr. Bland and Principal Sterling. And Minnesota Milo.

Fiona looked around. "Did I say that out loud?"

"Apparently," said Mr. Bland, clearing his throat.

"Is there something you wanted to say about Florida?"

"I was just thinking how Florida begins with *F* like Fiona," she explained, "the same way that Minnesota begins with an *M* like, you know, Milo?" Fiona's voice got softer as she got to the end of her explanation and realized how dumb she sounded. Why was it that the thoughts in her head seemed really smart until she said them out loud?

Everybody laughed again. Except for Mr. Bland and Principal Sterling. And Milo. They just stared at her.

Mr. Bland took a deep breath and sighed. Then he shook Milo's hand and said, "Welcome to Ordinary Elementary." He pointed to the empty desk next to Fiona's. "You can take your seat there."

As Milo reached his desk, he looked at Fiona and scowled. Fiona didn't know what she had done to deserve such a look from somebody she hadn't even talked to yet. But since she was not the kind of girl to let a scowl go unanswered, she shot back with an over-the-shoulder Doom Scowl, with medium doom.

"We're finishing up a lesson on measurements, and I'm afraid we won't have your books until later this week," Mr. Bland said to Milo. "But in the meantime, why don't you share with your neighbor?"

Milo looked at Fiona. He shook his head and then turned around to Harold Chutney at the desk behind him.

"Oh, Boise Idaho," said Harold, rubbing his nose, "you want to share with me?"

"I guess," said Milo.

"Cool beans," said Harold. "I like your hairdo. How do you get it to stand up—"

"Milo," said Mr. Bland, "you won't be able to see the chalkboard if you're turned around like that. Share with Fiona."

"Ugh," said Milo.

They grow them rotten in Minnesota, Fiona thought.

Milo moved his chair slowly toward Fiona. She moved her math book exactly one-half inch in Milo's direction. That was as far as she was going to go.

All during math, Milo turned the pages of Fiona's book before she was ready. And each time she turned them back, he mumbled something under his breath. Something that Fiona couldn't quite make out. Which made her grit her teeth.

The second math was over, Fiona pulled her book away, slammed it shut, and shoved it into her desk. Then she raised her hand. She couldn't wait any longer. "When are you going to draw names for classroom jobs?" she asked when Mr. Bland called on her.

Mr. Bland sighed. "Fiona, whatever would I do without you?" Only he didn't say it in a cursive-letters-on-a-greeting-card kind of way.

*   *   &   *   *

He said it in a way that made her think Mr. Bland knew exactly what he would do without her.

"And so I don't have to hear you ask a fourth time today," he said, "let's go ahead and draw the names now. But first we need to let Milo put his name in a bucket."

"Oh," said Fiona. She wasn't counting on that.

"Milo," said Mr. Bland, "there are several jobs available in this classroom. Courier, gardener, accountant, and so on. If you see a job you'd like to do, put your name on a piece of paper and drop it into that bucket. Each month we draw a new name."

Milo went over to the Job Center. Fiona chewed on her Thinking Pencil as she watched Milo read the duties listed under each job. He took a gazillion years. Finally, he wrote his name on a slip of paper and dropped it into the bucket marked ELECTRICIAN.

Rotten.

"And now for the big moment," said Mr. Bland, reaching into the first bucket marked COURIER. Fiona was busy crossing each of her fingers while Mr. Bland read off the names in each bucket. Only one bucket mattered to her.

"And lastly, classroom electrician," said Mr. Bland.

"Wait!" Fiona said, as her pinkie slipped off her ring finger. She quickly recrossed them. "Okay, now I'm ready." She watched Mr. Bland pull out a piece of paper and unfold it. As she watched, the corned beef feeling got so strong she could almost smell it.

Mr. Bland held up the paper. "Our new electrician is . . ." Fiona squeezed her crossed fingers tighter and whispered her own name. ". . . Milo Bridgewater."

Chapter 2

That does it," Fiona said to Cleo as they headed toward the bus circle after school. "Bring on the stink."

"Don't count on coming over to my house, then," said Cleo. "My mom keeps telling me that I need to wear air freshener. In my armpits."

Fiona stuck her nose up close and sniffed. "They don't smell bad to me."

"That's what I keep telling her."

Fiona took in a deep breath and let it out in a huff. "The worst thing isn't that I didn't get picked to be electrician. The worst thing is that Milo Bridgewater did. I've waited forever. And he gets picked on his first day!"

"No fair," said Cleo, pinching Fiona's arm. "But at least I get to be line leader."

She pinched Cleo's arm back. "Yeah, that's good at least."

"And Harold gets to be gardener."

"Yeah."

"Don't worry, Fiona," said Cleo, cracking her knuckles, one finger at a time. "I'll make sure Milo doesn't jump the lunch line."

Fiona half-smiled. Then she spotted an orange minivan in the parking lot. "There's the Bingo Bus. Bye."

As Fiona got closer to the minivan, she saw Mrs. Miltenberger waving at her from the driver's seat. Mrs. Miltenberger, an honorary grandmother to Fiona and her little brother, Max, was a part-time owner of the Bingo Bus.

As Fiona climbed onto the bus, the other part-time owners in the backseat—Mrs. Lordeau, Mrs. Huff, and Mrs. O'Brien—were talking over top of one another. They called themselves the Bingo Broads. Mostly because they loved playing bingo at the American Legion. They even had matching sweatshirts that said so in sparkles across the chest: BINGO RULES!

"That's when I decided it was time to get back in the dating game," Mrs. Lordeau was saying. "And that's how I met my Sandy."

"Good for you," said Mrs. O'Brien. "You've got to just get out there and meet people."

"That's what I keep telling Violet," said Mrs. Huff. "But does she hear me?"

"Oh, I hear you all right," said Mrs. Miltenberger. She winked at Fiona in the rearview mirror as Fiona settled into her middle-row seat. "How was your day?"

"Fine," Fiona said with a shrug.

"Oh, dear," said Mrs. O'Brien. "That doesn't sound good."

Fiona turned around in her seat to face them.

"No, it doesn't," added Mrs. Lordeau, cleaning her eyeglasses with her shirtsleeve. "Not good at all."

"What is it, sugar?" said Mrs. Huff. "Teacher problems? Homework problems?" Then she cleared her throat and said in a low voice, "Boy problems?"

Mrs. Lordeau slid her glasses back on her nose and leaned in close. "You can spill the beans to us, honey."

"Easy, girls," called Mrs. Miltenberger from the driver's seat. "Fiona, you don't have to put up with them for long. We've got only a few blocks to go to pick up Max from swim practice and then I'm dropping them all off at the Legion."

"You just watch the road, Violet," Mrs. O'Brien answered back, winking at Fiona. "We've got this handled."

Fiona wasn't used to telling the Bingo Broads her problems. But with her dad at the TV station a lot, where he was the chief meteorologist, and her mom living in California where she worked as an actress on the soap opera *Heartaches and Diamonds*, Fiona was glad to have grown-ups in arm's reach who were interested in hearing her troubles. "Well, I guess kind of boy problems," she said. "Sort of. I mean, there's one boy. And he's got problems."

"I knew it," said Mrs. Huff. "What did I tell you!"

Mrs. O'Brien nudged Mrs. Huff with her shoulder. "You're a genius, Betty. Now let her talk," she said. "Go on, Fiona."

Fiona told them about Milo Bridgewater, spiky hair and all, and how he scowled at her for no good reason and that just because he's a new kid from Minnesota, he can do anything he wants. Including being electrician.

Fiona paused to catch her breath and watched the Bingo Broads exchange sideways looks.

"I see," said Mrs. O'Brien. Mrs. Huff and Mrs. Lordeau nodded and said that they, too, saw.

"What do you see?" asked Fiona.

"Stepping on your toes a bit, is he?" said Mrs. O'Brien.

Fiona looked at her feet.

"This is the case of a boy just trying to fit in," explained Mrs. Huff.

"What you need to do," said Mrs. Lordeau, "is kick him with kindness. The sweeter you are, the sweeter he'll be."

"Gross. No way," declared Fiona. The kicking part wouldn't be a problem, but the kindness was not going to happen.

"She's right-o," added Mrs. O'Brien. "It's called the art of flattery. You can attract more flies with sugar than you can with vinegar."

"But I don't—" began Fiona, shaking her head.

Mrs. Huff interrupted. "It's honey, not sugar."

"What is?" asked Mrs. O'Brien.

"You said that you can attract more flies with sugar. But the saying goes, 'You can attract more flies with *honey*.' Honey. Not sugar."

"But . . ." Fiona tried again.

"You're both wrong," said Mrs. Lordeau. "It's bees. Not flies. 'You can attract more *bees* with honey.'"

"Why on earth would you want to attract bees?" said Mrs. O'Brien.

"Well, who wants a bunch of flies?" answered Mrs. Lordeau.

Fiona's brain felt like melted Velveeta. "I don't want to attract flies or bees," she said, louder than she should have. "I just wanted to be the one to plug in the TV, not Milo."

"I still say, kick him with kindness," said Mrs. Huff, pulling at the mole hair under her chin.

"I don't see how that would work," said Fiona.

"I've got an idea," said Mrs. O'Brien. "Let's try it on Max. What do you say, girls?"

◉ ◉ ◉ ◉

When they got to the YMCA, Max was waiting on the front steps. Fiona watched him from the window of the bus as he adjusted his goggles and hopped down the steps on the heels of his orange flippers. The towel that was tied around his neck like a cape swung to the side. Captain Seahorse.

He opened the door of the bus and announced, "Superhero on board, ladies!" He climbed in beside Fiona, who was still shaking her head.

"Afternoon, Captain," said Mrs. Miltenberger.

"Afternoon," he said. He grabbed the door handle with both hands and pulled on it to slide the door closed. But the door didn't budge.

"I've been meaning to grease that door," said Mrs. Huff. "It's been sticking something awful."

Fiona leaned over to help. "I can do it!" shouted Max, pushing her away.

Fiona looked at the Broads, who were nodding

and encouraging her with their eyes. She went over what they had told her in her head, and wasn't sure she could do it. In her head, the words were so sugary they made her lips pucker. But somehow, she forced them out. "Captain Seahorse," she said, swallowing hard, "your superhero muscles are probably tired from all of that swimming. I can help you." She swallowed again. "If you want."

The Bingo Broads nodded and smiled in approval.

Fiona felt sick. She truly almost gagged.

For a long moment, Max stared at her through his goggles. Then he said, "What's wrong with you? Why are you being so nice?" Which Fiona thought was a rude thing to say because, of all the big sisters she knew, she considered herself to be a pretty nice one. After all, she didn't tattle on him every day and only once in a while broke his crayons on purpose.

But then Max did something unexpected. He let go of the door handle and sat back in his seat. Fiona couldn't believe she had gotten her way. Without a fight or anything. She smiled to herself as she leaned over him and pulled the door closed.

• Chapter 3 •

Calling all snow angels," said Dad, knocking on the door to the dressing room at WORD-TV news station.

"Here I am," Fiona answered, opening the door. She pulled out her tutu as she followed him down the hallway and into his office. Fiona had been known as the station's snow angel ever since she gave her first weather report during one of Ordinary's biggest snowstorms. And now she reported on the weather a couple times a week.

Dad sat down at his desk and looked at the computer screen.

"Any snow on the way?" Fiona asked. She tugged at her costume's skirt to get it facing the right way and then started untwisting her shoulder straps. The tutu seemed to get smaller every time she put it on.

"Not this week, Dancing Bean," he said. He rolled over to her on his desk chair, which Fiona and Max named Turner, and helped her untwist.

"Is it ever going to snow again?" Fiona asked. She looked over at the computer screens on her dad's desk and frowned at the green blobs moving across the map.

Dad let go of her straps and patted her shoulders. "There you are. Right as rain." Then he rolled Turner back over to his keyboard, pressed a few keys, and pointed to the screen. "See this low-pressure system? It's moving in from the south and bringing up some warm air."

"Warm air?" complained Fiona. "But it's January. It's supposed to be cold. And snowy."

"This is winter in Maryland," said Dad.

"Ordinary," said Fiona with a sigh. Then for some reason Milo Bridgewater's scowly face flashed in her head. "I bet the weather in Minnesota is the same, though, right?"

"Minnesota?"

"Yeah," said Fiona. "I mean, the weather isn't any better there."

"Well, it depends what you mean by better," said Dad. He clicked some keys and brought up a map of the United States. He pointed to an area on the screen that was covered in pink. "This is Minnesota. And look at the size of the snow-storm they are having right now."

"No way!" said Fiona. "They have pink snow in Minnesota?"

Dad gave her a look.

"Just kidding," she said. Only, she was just

half-kidding. Part of her believed that if Milo could be picked as electrician on his first day in a new school, he just might be lucky enough to be from a place that snowed pink snowflakes.

"Right," said Dad. "Good one."

"It snows a lot there?"

"You betcha," he said. "Sometimes four to five feet at a time."

Fiona huffed. "Lucky."

"And it can get down to fifty degrees below freezing. Talk about weather that's not ordinary. It's extraordinary."

"Extraordinary." Fiona said it real slow. She knew the word because she got it wrong on Mr. Bland's vocabulary test a couple of weeks ago. By the looks of it, you would think "extraordinary" meant extra ordinary. Like extra ketchup. Extra large. Extra snowy. But it really meant the opposite of ordinary. It was another one of those lying kind of words.

● ● ● ●

At school the next day, Mr. Bland still didn't have Milo's books. Fiona had to do more sharing.

"Hey, Florida. What's with the Halloween costume?" Milo whispered during their history lesson.

Fiona looked at the flared jeans and striped T-shirt she was wearing. "Huh?"

"On TV last night," said Milo. "I saw your weather report."

"Oh, that. It's called a tutu," said Fiona. "I take ballet. And it's Fiona, not Florida."

Mr. Bland tapped the chalkboard. "Who can tell me what the word 'declaration' means? Anybody?"

Fiona pulled at her eyebrow. She had discovered that if she could pull out just one hair, Mr. Bland wouldn't call on her. But if she pulled out two, or even three hairs, she was going to get called on for sure. She yanked. One hair.

"Cleo," said Mr. Bland.

"It means an announcement," she said. History was Cleo's best subject. She had the kind of brain that was good at remembering dates of wars and names of presidents, which was all history seemed to be, anyway. Fiona's brain was not so good at remembering those kinds of things.

"Exactly," said Mr. Bland. "An announcement. A formal statement about something important." Mr. Bland picked up a pile of papers from his desk. "Who is our classroom courier this month?" Leila Rad raised her hand. "Oh, right, Leila. Would you please pass out these worksheets?"

Fiona took a worksheet from Leila and chewed on her Thinking Pencil.

"Whatever," whispered Milo.

"Are you still talking to me?" asked Fiona.

"What does a tutu have to do with the weather?" He made a face when he said the word "tutu" like he had just bit into cauliflower.

"I'm the snow angel." Fiona explained how she was an angel in *The Nutcracker* and how on the night of the performance there was a huge snowstorm, and how she went on the air IN A TUTU to report on it to keep her dad from getting into trouble. She smiled, remembering.

"That's dumb," he said. "Does it ever even snow here?"

"It is not dumb," said Fiona, trying hard to keep her voice low. "And I just told you that we had a big snowstorm. So Y-E-S it snows here."

"No talking," said Mr. Bland. "You've got about ten minutes to get started on the worksheet before we move on to a Declaration of Independence video."

"A few inches, big deal," whispered Milo.

"Shush," said Fiona.

"This place is nothing like Minnesota."

Fiona was just about to ask Milo why he doesn't go back to Minnesota if it's so flat-out great, when she remembered what the Bingo Broads told her about kicking him with kindness. Or keeping flies away from your food while the bees are busy with their honey. Or something like that.

Fiona started kicking. "So," she said quietly, "Minnesota must be a whole lot better than here, huh?"

Milo raised his eyebrows. "What do you mean?"

"I mean, it gets colder than zero there?"

"Yeah," he said.

"I saw on TV once where it was so cold that some guy's toes fell right off," said Fiona. "When he left the house, all of his toes were on, but when he got to work half of them were off." She wiggled her toes. "I forget where it happened, but it was probably Minnesota. Pretty cool."

Milo shrugged. He looked like he wasn't familiar with toe-losing weather. Maybe it wasn't Minnesota after all.

"Sometimes it gets so cold that spit freezes as soon as it hits the sidewalk," said Milo.

"Gross."

Milo rolled his eyes. "One time, on a real cold day, my friend back home could get his spit to *bounce*. It's not gross. It's great."

"Oh, that's what I meant." This was the first time Fiona ever had a conversation about spit, and she didn't know what to say about it. Then she thought for a moment and came up with: "I really love spit."

Milo gave her a look.

Fiona changed the subject. "I heard that it snows four feet at a time there."

"Sometimes more than that."

"I mean, whoa," said Fiona, making her voice sound extra impressed. She couldn't tell for sure, but she thought he might have even smiled just then. Fiona could hardly believe it, but this kicking thing was working. "You must have had off from school all the time."

Milo just looked at her. "Why do you say that?"

It took a lot for Fiona to not say *duh*. "You

know," she said, "because of all the snow there."

Milo's smile disappeared. "No. We're so used to the snow that we hardly ever have off from school," he said.

"Truth?" she said. Fiona never imagined there was a place where everything didn't stop when it snowed. "We have snow days here even when there is only a couple of inches on the ground. And sometimes they close school even before it starts to snow."

Milo crossed his arms. "So what? Big deal."

"I didn't mean—"

"Who cares?" said Milo.

"Don't you like to have off from school?" asked Fiona.

He shrugged and turned away, mumbling something again.

"What?" Fiona didn't know what she said wrong, but all this kicking with kindness was making her grouchy. She was ready to give Milo one more kick—a real one—when Mr. Bland said, "Let's move on to the Declaration of Independence video. We need our classroom electrician. Milo?"

Fiona's cheeks burned as she watched Milo plug in the TV and DVD player and press the buttons on the remote control. She stuck her hand up in the air and waved it at Mr. Bland.

"What is it, Fiona?"

"Can I turn out the lights?"

"It's up to Milo to pick an assistant electrician for that task, if he wants," said Mr. Bland.

At least a gazillion other hands shot up into the air, including Cleo's and Harold's. Fiona kept her hand up and waved it back and forth at Milo.

Milo looked around the room and scratched his chin just like a villain from a whodunit on TV. His eyes stopped on Fiona. He smiled. She smiled back and waved even faster at him. "I pick Harold," he said.

Fiona dropped her hand in disgust. "Fine," she declared, trying to put lots of splinters on the word and hoping that Milo felt every one of them.

Chapter 4

Y

ou were right, Fiona," said Harold as they got off the school bus. "Electrician is the best job."

Fiona rolled her eyes. "You were only the *assistant* electrician."

"I know, but I got to turn off the lights," he said. "And turn them back on again."

"So?" said Fiona. "I turn lights on and off all the time at home."

"Are you sure it's okay if I stay at your house

until my grandma picks me up?" Harold asked, following Fiona up the walkway to her house.

"I told you a gazillion times that it's fine," she snapped. "Didn't I?"

"Oh, Boise Idaho," said Harold. "Somebody ate a bowl of Nasties today."

Fiona scratched her head again. Her brain felt itchy from all the mean words that were swirling around trying to get out.

"Milo said he's going to start a club at school," said Harold.

Fiona bit her lip and kept walking.

"Milo and his older brother started an explorer's club when they lived in Minnesota," he said. "Don't you think that would be buckets of fun?"

She pressed her lips together tight and climbed the steps to her front porch.

"Harold Chutney, explorer and adventure-seeker," he said, looking up into the sky like he was watching himself on a giant movie screen.

Then he pulled at his hair with his hands, forcing it to stand straight up. Like Milo's. "Can't you see it?"

Fiona couldn't see it. Not at all. She put both hands on Harold's head and pressed until his hair was flat again.

"Ow!" said Harold.

"Milo. Milo. Milo!" she yelled. "Who flat-out cares about Milo Bridgewater?" Then she opened the front door and marched inside.

"Jeez Louise, Fiona," said Harold, following her. He put his finger up his nose. "You didn't have to yell."

When the words came out of her mouth, Fiona felt better and worse at the same time. Mostly worse. "Sorry, Harold." She led him into the kitchen and pulled down a jar of peanut butter from the cupboard. She stuck her finger into the jar, pulled out a glob of peanut butter, and put it in her mouth. Right away the peanut butter wrapped up her troubles in a tiny box and mailed it to the moon.

Harold reached his finger toward the jar.

Fiona held the jar out to him and then pulled it away. "Wait," she said, staring at his finger. "You need a spoon."

"You look different today," said Harold.

Fiona looked at herself. "I do?"

"And you smell a little different too."

Fiona sniffed her armpits. "Awesome!" She

couldn't wait to see what Mr. Bland had to say about her stink.

She let Harold have the last spoonful to make up for the Nasties. "How do you know all that stuff about Milo?"

Harold licked the spoon like a lollipop. "Are you going to yell at me again?"

"No, Harold. Jeez."

"He told me at recess."

"Oh."

"Maybe we can be in Milo's club." Harold handed her the spoon and she laid it on the countertop.

"I'm not sure I'm an explorer kind of girl," said Fiona.

"Oh, he's not starting an explorer's club," said Harold.

"But you said—"

"That was in Minnesota," said Harold. "Milo said he was going to start a different kind of club here."

"What kind?" asked Fiona.

"A meteorology club."

"A what?" Fiona could not believe her ears. "But I'm the . . . but that's my . . . he can't . . ."

The phone rang then.

"Hello, Fiona sweetheart," said Mom. "I was wondering if I'd get to talk to you. I thought you might be at ballet."

Fiona was still thinking about what Harold just told her. Electricity wasn't enough for Milo, now he was going to take the weather away from her too? Mrs. O'Brien was right. Milo Bridgewater was stepping on her toes. Except that he wasn't just stepping. He was flat-out dancing on them.

"Fiona?" said Mom. "Are you there?"

"Gah" was all that came out of Fiona's mouth.

"I was saying that I thought you might be at ballet."

"Ballet is over until it starts back up again, remember?" Having a mom who lived all the way in California meant she forgot the things that happened all the way on this side of the country.

"Oh, that's right. I think you mentioned that," she said. "So what's new, wonderful, and exciting in Ordinary?"

"Nothing," said Fiona. "Except for a new boy at school who is taking over everything. And he hates my guts. And my tutu."

"I'm sure he doesn't," said Mom. "How could anyone hate you? You are lovely." Which is what moms have to say because it is the law. Fiona knew it wasn't always the truth. After all, Fiona had heard the nice things her mom said about Max.

"You know what my mother always told me," Mom said.

"What?" asked Fiona.

"Boys only pick on girls they like."

"Why would someone be mean to someone they liked?" Fiona asked Mrs. Miltenberger, as she watched her slide a pan of lasagna into the oven.

"That's the million-dollar question," said Mrs.

Miltenberger. She closed the oven door and flung a tea towel across her shoulder. "Harold, honey, your grandma's stuck at work, so you're staying for dinner."

Harold gave her the okay sign and said, "What's the million-dollar answer?"

"If I knew that, I'd have a house in Tahiti." Mrs. Miltenberger picked up the empty jar of peanut butter from the counter. "Rough day?"

Fiona nodded.

Mrs. Miltenberger looked her over. "When is the last time you had a bath, young lady?"

"Four days ago," said Fiona. "I'm done with baths until Mr. Bland picks me to be electrician."

"I don't know what that means," said Mrs. Miltenberger, "but you've got a date with the tub tonight. There will be no dirty girls or boys in this house. No, sir."

Fiona huffed. Why were grown-ups always getting in the way of her plans?

"Can I have a glass of milk?" yelled Max from the living room.

"If you come in here and get it," answered Mrs. Miltenberger.

Max waddled into the kitchen on the heels of his flippers. "Milk me," he said in his Captain Seahorse voice.

"I thought you were Captain Seahorse, not Captain Seacow," said Fiona, and Harold snorted.

Max cocked his head. "I don't get it." He took the glass from Mrs. Miltenberger with both hands and gulped it down.

"So," said Mrs. Miltenberger. She sat down at the kitchen table across from Fiona and Harold. "Where were we?"

"A question that costs a million big ones," said Harold.

"Right," said Mrs. Miltenberger. "A long time ago, when I was a sweet young thing—and don't look so surprised because as I said, it was a long time ago."

Fiona and Harold looked at each other. Fiona forced her eyebrows to lower, and Mrs. Miltenberger continued. "Anyway, when I first met Mr. Miltenberger, rest his soul, I wouldn't give him the time of day. I'm not exaggerating. He would ask me for the time, and even though I always wore the Timex that my mother and father had given me for a high school graduation present, I wouldn't tell him." She smiled and then tapped her chin with her finger. "I wonder whatever happened to that watch."

"Why wouldn't you tell him what time it was?" Fiona asked. "Didn't you like him?"

"Did I like him?" repeated Mrs. Miltenberger. "He was the only boy that could make strudel as good as my mother's and knew how to do his own laundry."

"My grandma showed me how to make strudel," said Harold.

"And you're a catch," said Mrs. Miltenberger, with a wink.

"Then why were you mean to him?" asked Fiona. "To Mr. Miltenberger, I mean."

"What are you all talking about?" asked Max, wiping away his milk mustache with his bare arm.

"*Amore*," said Mrs. Miltenberger.

"Huh?"

"Love," she said.

"I'm out of here," said Max, handing the empty glass to Mrs. Miltenberger and waddling away.

"Wait a second," said Fiona. "Love? Gross! I'm in fourth grade. Nobody is talking about . . . I can't even say it. L-O-V-E. Yuck."

• Chapter 5 •

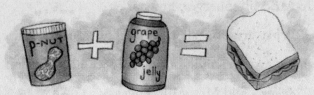

iona had to stand on her head and sing "On Top of Spaghetti" twice all the way through to get Mrs. Miltenberger's gross-out L-O-V-E talk out of her brain. *Bleck*. And she had to stay in the bathtub for a gazillion years until she passed Mrs. Miltenberger's stink test.

Fiona hoped that Harold had gotten it all wrong about Milo's club. After all, Harold got confused about things almost as much as Fiona did. Like the one time when he thought that dust bunnies were a real kind of rabbit that lived under the couch.

She figured he could be wrong about this, too.

But at school, a gigantic poster hanging on the back of the classroom door proved that Harold could be right some of the time.

METEOROLOGY ROCKS!

WHAT:
Meteorology Club

WHEN:
Tomorrow after school

WHERE:
Mr. Bland's 4th-grade classroom

WHY:
Weather can be cool, and so can you.

WHO:
Milo, club president
(No costumes allowed.)

Fiona had heard people on TV say that when they got mad they saw red. Just like bulls did when they saw a red cape. Until now, Fiona had wondered if that was real. But the more she looked at Milo's poster, Fiona was certain. She had the urge to snort and stomp her feet and charge. . . . Did her itchy brain mean that horns were growing?

It didn't help that everybody in Mr. Bland's classroom was talking about joining Milo's stupid club. Fiona couldn't figure out why they were suddenly interested in meteorology. They thought that meteorology had to do with outer space before she had set them straight.

Besides, it was Fiona's dad, not Milo's, who was the chief meteorologist at the news station. And it was Fiona, not Milo, who was on TV giving weather reports. Nobody seemed to care about the weather before. But now, all of a sudden, Milo from Minnesota was the weather superstar?

Fiona didn't talk to Milo all morning. And Fiona was glad that his books finally came in, because she was all done with sharing.

"The world has really gone mixed-up," Fiona said to Cleo in the lunch line. "I feel like a fruit smoothie."

Cleo walked up and down the line checking to make sure everybody had their lunchboxes and milk money. "And did you see what his poster says?" Fiona said when Cleo came back to the front of the line. "The part about the costume?"

Cleo nodded. But Fiona could tell she was more bothered about being line leader. Fiona looked at Milo at the end of the lunch line. He was talking and laughing with Harold and Leila Rad and others.

She scratched her head. And then she marched right over to him. "What's the part about 'no costumes allowed' supposed to mean?"

Harold picked at the tip of his nose. "Hi, Fiona."

She growled "hi" back and folded her arms

across her chest. "That's supposed to be about me and my tutu, isn't it?" she said to Milo.

Milo shrugged, all innocent-like. And that made Fiona grit her teeth. "Principal Sterling told me after she saw my first weather report on TV that I should start a meteorology club, you know," she said.

Milo raised his eyebrows. "So why didn't you?"

That stung. "What? Well . . . but . . . you're only starting this club because you saw me on TV doing the weather."

"You're not the boss of the weather," said Leila Rad, twirling a strand of her dark hair around her fingertip.

"Yeah," said the other kids.

"But . . ." said Fiona. Didn't they see? Milo didn't care about the weather. The only thing he cared about was making her miserable. *Maybe Mom was right,* she thought.

"Why would I start a club just because I saw you on TV?" said Milo.

And in front of everybody, Fiona said to him, "Because, Milo. Because I think you like me. I think you *like*-like me. And that's why you are so mean."

Milo's face got Valentine's Day red. "You think I *like*-like you?"

Fiona nodded. She looked at all of the surprised

faces around her. Including Milo's. They started laughing then, and Fiona wondered how she could be so sure of something one minute, and the next minute, what she was so sure of didn't make any sense at all. "You don't?"

In the front seat of the Dingo Dus, Fiona sat quietly, thinking. Why were grown-ups always giving her bad advice? When Fiona had stage fright, Mrs. Miltenberger told her to picture the audience in their underwear when she felt nervous. But when she tested the experiment on Mr. Bland, her giggles got her sent to the principal's office. Then, just the other day, the Bingo Broads told her to kick Milo with kindness, but that didn't even get her the job of assistant electrician. And then Fiona's mom told her that boys only pick on girls they like. Well, that was the whopper of them all.

What's the point of being a grown-up if they don't know any more than I do? Fiona wondered. She decided that she would be better off on her own. Just like in the olden days when all those colonials signed the Declaration of Independence. They were tired of getting bad advice from the king of England, and they told him so. Plus, she bet they didn't have to take baths if they didn't want to.

After they picked up Max from swim practice and were heading to the American Legion, Fiona knew what she had to do. "I am making a declaration of independence," she announced. "I am never following another grown-up's advice as long as I live. From now on, I'm on my own. Independent."

"Oh, my," said Mrs. Miltenberger from the driver's seat. "We've steered you wrong?"

"That's right," said Fiona.

"It's an uprising," said Mrs. Lordeau.

"She's gone indie on us," said Mrs. Huff.

"Flying the coop," said Mrs. O'Brien.

"Me too," declared Max, chewing on a corner of his towel cape. "I'm done with grown-ups."

"What happened to you?" Fiona asked.

"Coach wants me to learn the breaststroke," said Max.

Fiona shook her head. A six-year-old's problems were small potatoes. "What's wrong with that?"

"I can't do the breaststroke," said Max. "I'm no good at it."

"But you're the best dolphin on your team," said Mrs. Miltenberger. "Maybe you just need to—"

"Don't listen to them, Max," said Fiona. She quickly grabbed his hands and put them over his ears. Then she covered her ears with her hands and kept them there the whole ride home.

• Chapter 6 •

Fiona chewed on her green Thinking Pencil with the fierceness and underbite of a bulldog. She spit out the bits of wood that came from thinking too hard. *First there was electrician and now meteorology. What was next? Ballet?* Fiona had to admit, Milo doing a *pirouette* would be hilarious.

"If you don't mind me saying so," said Mrs. Miltenberger, sitting next to Fiona and Max on the couch, "and this isn't really advice, so I'm not interfering with your declaration of independence, I don't think. But if you keep chewing like that, you could break a tooth. Or get a splinter in your tongue."

Fiona chewed harder. Until her pencil snapped in half. "I've got it!" she said, removing the pieces from her mouth. Milo seemed to like being a toe-stepper. Maybe she should be a toe-stepper too. *A toe-flattener.* "I'm going to start my own club." It was her second declaration of the day, and it tasted like melted marshmallows on toast.

"Sounds like a bold idea to me," said Mrs. Miltenberger. "Now, does your newly declared independence include dinner? Or are you still counting on grown-ups for that?"

"Grown-ups are still good for food," said Fiona. "And I'm starved."

"Yeah, same for me," said Max.

"Well," said Mrs. Miltenberger, "it's in the oven, and I've got to get ready for my date."

"Your *what*?" said Fiona.

"Let's not make a big deal out of it," said Mrs. Miltenberger.

"Who's your date?" Fiona asked.

Max pulled his goggles off his head. "Yeah, who?"

Mrs. Miltenberger straightened a stack of magazines on the coffee table. "I don't know. The Broads fixed me up with him." She rubbed the back of her neck. "I don't know why in tarnation I ever agreed to this." She shook her head and waved her hands. "Anyway, since your father is working at the station tonight, I've arranged for a babysitter—sorry, I mean *watcher*—for you."

When she was in second grade, Fiona decided that she did not like the word "babysitter" when it had anything to do with her. After all, she no longer considered herself to be a *baby*, and she did not ever wish to be *sat*. Instead, Fiona thought "watcher" was a more acceptable word. The watcher could watch Fiona and Max and play games with them, and while watching over them, make sure they did not get kidnapped by gypsies or turn on scary movies that you think you want to watch but afterward wish you hadn't.

"Not Mrs. Huff again," said Fiona. Mrs. Huff was crazy about horror movies. But she was too much of a scaredy cat to watch them by herself, and she liked to cling to Fiona and Max.

"Not after the *Zombie Revenge VII* incident," said Mrs. Miltenberger. "I've promised your father that Mrs. Huff will not be sitting—er, watching—you ever again."

The doorbell rang just then, before Fiona could ask the name of the new watcher. She got to the door two seconds behind Max.

He swung open the door. "There's a girl I don't know standing here!"

A teenager, a cool-looking one with high-top sneakers, hooped earrings, and a chained wallet stood in the open doorway. "You're not supposed

to open the door until you know who it is," Fiona
reminded Max.

"Fine," said Max, shutting the door. Then he
yelled into it. "Who is it?"

"Max!" yelled Fiona.

"It's Loretta Gormley," said the teenager through the door.

"It's Betty Wormly!" said Max. He opened the door, made a face at Fiona, and went back to the couch.

"Loretta, don't mind him," said Mrs. Miltenberger from behind Fiona. She shot Max a disapproving look. "Come in, come in. These are your charges for tonight—Fiona and Max."

Max cleared his throat and scowled at Mrs. Miltenberger. "Okay, right. Sorry, I mean, Captain Seahorse."

Loretta Gormley took off her jean jacket and sank into the couch. She smiled at Fiona. Fiona was already smiling. A real, true-to-life teenager was going to be her watcher.

"Want to play Squidman?" Max asked Fiona.

"No."

"You never play with me anymore," said Max.

"I do too."

"Do not," he said louder.

"Do too. Infinity." Fiona glared at him. Max huffed and crawled under the coffee table.

Fiona sat down beside Loretta on the couch. "What grade are you in?"

"Eleventh."

"Cool," said Fiona.

"Yeah." Loretta took her cell phone out of her corduroy purse and looked at it.

"I'm in fourth grade."

"Cool," said Loretta Gormley, pulling up her feet onto the couch so she was sitting like a pretzel.

"Yeah." *This was going great.*

"Are you in any clubs?" Fiona asked Loretta, making her legs into a pretzel.

"I'm in the Hospitality League," she said. "We volunteer at nursing homes. And I'm a Knitwit. We knit scarves and hats for the homeless. And S.M.U.G.S."

"What's that?"

"Students Majorly United for a Greener School," said Loretta. "I'm totally all about helping people, you know? Making the world a better place."

"Cool," said Fiona.

"Yeah." Loretta looked at her phone again and sighed.

"I'm starting my own club," said Fiona.

"Cool."

"Why do you keep looking at your phone?" asked Fiona.

"When somebody tells you he's going to call you, he should call. Not that I'm, like, all about sitting around and waiting for him, but it's common courtesy, you know? I mean, if I say I'm like going to do something, I do it. Am I right?"

Fiona nodded. Their conversation had somehow gone off the road and into the woods, leaving her lost. Teenagers were so mysterious.

"Anyway, do you want to know what kind of club I'm starting?" asked Fiona.

"Sure," said Loretta.

"It's called the Society for Not-so-Ordinary Weather," said Fiona. "S.N.O.W."

"A meteorology club?" said Loretta.

"Yep."

Chapter 7

Late into the night, Fiona worked on her club poster. She loaded it with sparkles and glitter and giant paper snowflakes.

Once the poster was done, Fiona designed a snowsuit. She turned her Enchanted Forest T-shirt inside out and then wrote "S.N.O.W." in glitter paint across the front. She painted over the blue stripe on her white sneakers and dug out her white cargo pants.

• • • •

Let it S.N.O.W.!!!

The Society for Not-so-Ordinary Weather
(AKA: S.N.O.W.)
will meet today after school.
No two snowflakes are alike, so...
Join the club that's not just cool...
it's flat-out cold!
32 degrees, actually.
The perfect temperature for snow days!
(Costumes allowed and encouraged!)

Fiona taped her poster to the wall of Mr. Bland's classroom, right beside Milo's. Then she handed out paper snowflakes. Each one had "Let it S.N.O.W.!" written on it in silver glitter ink. "Take one and pass it on," she said.

"What is this supposed to be?" asked Milo.

"It's a snowflake," answered Fiona.

"Duh," said Milo. "I meant, what are they for?"

Fiona ignored him and then raised her hand.

"Yes, Fiona?" said Mr. Bland.

"Can I make an announcement?"

"That depends," said Mr. Bland.

"It has to do with school," said Fiona. "I promise."

Mr. Bland nodded and Fiona went to the front of the classroom. "You are all invited to the first meeting of the Society for Not-so-Ordinary Weather after school today." She pointed to her shirt. "I'm president."

"But Milo's club is meeting today," said Harold.

"Yeah, we can't have two meteorology clubs," said Milo.

Mr. Bland cleared his throat. "Milo makes a good point, Fiona. You know, you could combine your clubs and be co-presidents."

"No way," said Fiona and Milo at the same time. Fiona looked from Milo to Mr. Bland. "My club isn't a meteorology club, exactly," she said. "It's a club to predict snow days." She waited for a big *ta-da* reaction, but it didn't come.

"Well," said Mr. Bland, "we'll have to sort this out later."

"Can I still have my meeting today after school?" asked Fiona.

"But that's the same time as my club meeting," said Milo.

Mr. Bland waved his hands in the air. "For today only, you can both have your club meetings. I think this classroom is big enough to share. And we'll sort out the business of two weather clubs another time. Now, let's get going with fractions."

Fiona and Cleo stopped kids in the hallway, the cafeteria, and on the playground and reminded them about that day's S.N.O.W. meeting.

"I already told Milo I would join his club," most of them said.

"Well, what did you go and do a thing like *that* for?" asked Fiona. Nobody had a very good answer.

By the end of the school day, Fiona was afraid nobody except for Cleo and Harold would want to join her club. It would be just like gym class where nobody picked her first for kickball: Fiona Finkelstein, odd girl out.

When the last bell rang, Fiona sat at her desk with her head propped in her hands. Cleo hopped up on Fiona's desk and started cracking her knuckles. They both watched as Milo pulled things—lots of things—out of a box and spread them out on the reading table. She didn't want him to catch her staring and think she was interested, but she did see a thermometer, a barometer, and some kind of wooden stick.

Fiona looked at her empty desk. She didn't have things in a box. She didn't have a box.

Kids started to trickle in through the door, and
like magnets, they were pulled to Milo's table.
Even Harold was being sucked in. Some people had
magnetic appeal, Fiona knew, but she had never seen
it in action before. She thought magnetic appeal
had been along the lines of things like hearts of
gold and green thumbs—just things people said,

but weren't exactly real. But now she wasn't so sure.

"Harold," said Fiona, "the S.N.O.W. meeting is over here."

"Milo's got one of those Canadian weather sticks that tells you what the weather is going to be like," said Harold.

"Cool," said Cleo as she slid off Fiona's desk toward Milo.

"Hey," said Fiona, giving her a look.

"Well, they are," said Cleo. "I saw them on TV. They point toward the sky when the weather is nice and they point to the ground when it's not."

She was losing Harold and Cleo. Apparently, she did not have even one ounce of magnetic appeal. Any chance of having her own meteorology club was disappearing before her eyes. And what's worse, Milo Bridgewater was taking it from her.

"There's another club over here," Fiona shouted

at everyone on the other side of the room. She twirled and jumped and then dropped to the floor.

"Is she okay?" asked Milo.

"She's a snowflake," said Cleo.

Fiona jumped to her feet and curtsied.

"Your club is just about snow days?" said Milo.

Fiona nodded. "That's right."

"What does your club do when winter's over?"

"What do you mean?" said Fiona.

"When there are no more snow days to predict because it's springtime," he said.

Oh. Fiona hadn't thought that far ahead.

Chapter 8

Fiona trailed behind the grocery cart at Foodland while Mrs. Miltenberger fought with Max over a bag of Choco P. Nutters. Fiona stayed out of it. She knew better than to get involved in a battle with Max in the candy aisle, and besides, she had some battles of her own to figure out.

Like her war with Milo Bridgewater. Fiona wasn't giving up. She wasn't that kind of girl. And she wasn't giving in, either. Milo was right about one thing. It didn't make sense to have a club just about snow days. Not when winter was almost over anyway. She would just have to start another club. But what kind of club exactly?

Besides ballet, Fiona didn't know what she was good at. She liked giving weather reports okay, because it made her feel like sprinkles on plain ice cream: something special. But now that Milo was Mr. Weather Boy, she felt like a corner of mold on a slice of cheese: gross and green. And ordinary. What she really wanted, she knew, was to be *extraordinary* at something.

By the time they got to the end of the aisle and were turning the corner toward the canned vegetables, the bag of Choco P. Nutters was in the cart next to Max. "Okay, mister," said Mrs. Miltenberger, shaking a finger at Max. "For every junk thing your sticky fingers grab off the shelves, I'm putting in two very large amounts of vegetables for your dinner." Then she grabbed two cans off the shelf, giant-size ones, and handed them to Fiona. "These ought to do it." And she grinned as she said the word: "Succotash."

Max pulled his cape over his head.

"*I* don't have to eat this, do I?" asked Fiona. She could barely hold the cans with both hands, they were so heavy with bad-tasting vegetables.

"Nope," said Mrs. Miltenberger. "They're both for Max."

Before they even got past the canned peas, Max gave up. "Here," he said, holding out the bag to Mrs. Miltenberger.

"Wise decision," she said. "Fiona, you can put those back."

"What is succotash, anyway?" Fiona asked.

"Lima beans and corn."

"Huh?" said Fiona. "Lima beans and corn are already vegetables on their own. When you eat them together, why are they called something else?"

"I'm not sure," said Mrs. Miltenberger. "I guess they like each other's company." Mrs. Miltenberger's cell phone rang just then and Max hummed along to "Wouldn't It Be Loverly" while she dug through her pocketbook to find it. She pulled it out, looked at it and said, "Uck, the Broads." Then she dumped the phone back into her bag and pushed the cart onward.

"Why aren't you talking to them?" Fiona asked.

"It's going to be quite a while before I forgive them for last night's fix-up," she said. "A *mix-up* is more like it. It was quite possibly—and I'm not exaggerating here—the *worst* date on record."

"Did he have food stuck in his mustache?" asked Fiona. That's what always seemed to happen in bad dates on TV.

"Unfortunately nothing as interesting as that," said Mrs. Miltenberger. "Let's just say that the best part of the whole evening was when he nodded off at the restaurant and I paid the bill."

"Yikes."

"You're telling me," said Mrs. Miltenberger,

picking up a can of asparagus. "But don't you worry, I've learned my lesson. Despite their claims to the contrary, the Broads are no matchmakers. Too bad." She sighed. "Max, hold on, we're turning a corner."

Fiona wondered how people got together at all. She had never given it much thought before. She knew her mom and dad had been partnered up at Ordinary's Annual Square Dancing Jamboree a long time ago, so she figured everybody ended up together that way. Or something like it. A couple of *swing your partner and dos-i-dos!* and that would be it.

But if it didn't work that way for everybody, then how did people get matched up? As Fiona looked over the shelves of peanut butter jars and jellies, an idea began to grow in her brain. "How did peanut butter and jelly get together?"

"What?" said Mrs. Miltenberger.

"Did peanut butter always go with jelly?" said Fiona. "I mean, how did they meet?"

"Why on earth do you want to know that?"

Fiona shrugged.

"Well, let's see. This one I think I know. I'm pretty sure it happened in the 1940s, during World War Two," said Mrs. Miltenberger. "The soldiers thought they'd be good together."

"Huh," said Fiona. "So a soldier took a look at peanut butter and then took a look at jelly, and then he matched them up."

Mrs. Miltenberger raised her eyebrows at Fiona. "I guess you could put it that way. A match made in sandwich heaven."

"What do you get when you match these two?" asked Max, holding up a bottle of soy sauce and a tub of ice cream.

"Indigestion," answered Mrs. Miltenberger.

Up and down the grocery aisles, Fiona thought about things that went together. Then she knew what her new club was going to be.

❂ ❂ ❂ ❂

"Yes, Fiona?" said Mr. Dland, rubbing his forehead.

"Can I make an announcement?"

"Another one?"

"It has to do with my club," said Fiona.

"Quickly," he said. "We've got a lot to cover today."

Fiona stood at her desk. "I wanted to tell you that I'm starting a new club." She saw Cleo's mouth fall open, and Fiona could tell that she had everyone's attention. Including Milo's. "It's a club that meets when winter is over, or is about to be over. Basically, when everybody's tired of snow. Sort of like now. Anyway, the name of the club is the After-Winter Society of Ordinary Matchmakers. Otherwise known as A.W.S.O.M.M."

· Chapter 9 ·

Fiona unwrapped her sandwich at lunch and pulled apart the bread. "Peanut butter and jelly!" she said. "Extraordinary!"

"Have you been snatched by little green people from outer space and had your brain switched over?" said Cleo.

"I don't think so," said Fiona. "But my brain has been a little itchy."

"First you tell Milo Bridgewater, in front of everybody, that you think he *like*-likes you. Then you start a S.N.O.W. club without telling anybody, not even me. And now you've changed it into a club about matchmaking? It sounds a little outer spacey to me."

Ever since Milo got here, Fiona thought things did seem a little outer spacey.

"I think I'm going to try to eat with Milo at his table," said Harold, holding his tray of food.

"How come?" said Fiona. "I'll give you my carrot sticks."

"I've got a pork chop," said Cleo.

"No, thanks."

Fiona and Cleo watched Harold walk over to Milo's table. He walked around the table once and then turned around and came back.

"What happened?" asked Fiona.

Harold sat his tray down beside Fiona. "Nothing. I'll try another time. Can I still have that pork chop?"

Cleo gave it to him.

"I've been thinking," said Fiona, putting her bag of carrot sticks on Harold's tray.

"Here we go," said Cleo, shaking her head.

"To get people to join my matchmaking club," she said, "we need to show that I'm a good match-maker."

"How do we do that?" asked Harold with a mouthful of chewed chop.

"Yeah," said Cleo. "Don't even think about matching me up."

"We aren't going to match just *people*," said Fiona.

Harold picked at his nose. "I don't get it."

"Think of something you want," said Fiona. "Something to be matched up with."

Harold reached into his pants pocket and pulled out a folded piece of paper.

"What's that?" asked Fiona.

"My toy list."

Cleo and Fiona looked at each other.

"Every time I see a toy I want, I write it on the list," said Harold. "That way I won't forget. Don't you keep one?"

Fiona and Cleo shook their heads. Fiona had to admit, it wasn't such a bad idea. "Toys aren't matches," she said. "I mean, think of something you want that isn't a toy."

"I want a little brother or sister," said Cleo.

"You do? Why?" More than once, Fiona wanted to give Max away. Or sell him.

"I want to be popular like Milo," said Harold, finger in his nose.

Fiona tapped her finger to her chin. "Okay, fine," she said. "As president of A.W.S.O.M.M., I declare you Cleo Button, and you, Harold Chutney, are about to be matched."

"Up here!" called Fiona from her room. When Cleo and Harold appeared at her door, she pointed to her beanbag chair. She grabbed a handful of confetti from her party drawer and shoved it in her pocket. "Harold, sit. I will be right back." She found Max in his room and dragged him down the hall.

"Hey, let go," Max said. "Fiona!"

Fiona brought him to her room and said, "Do you want to play Squidman?"

"Is this a trick?"

"No trick," said Fiona, smiling.

Max looked at Fiona and then at Harold and Cleo behind her. "Okay."

"Okay, good," said Fiona. She took Cleo's hand and then put it into Max's.

"Huh?" said Cleo.

"You said you wanted a little brother or sister," said Fiona. She reached into her pocket and threw the confetti into the air. "Congratulations. It's a boy!"

"Fiona!" yelled Cleo.

"What's going on?" said Max.

"Number one match made," she said smiling.

"Max, Cleo is your big sister for today. I thought you wanted to play Squidman."

"All right, let's go," said Max, pulling Cleo down the hall.

Cleo's face turned red but she didn't say a word. It felt good to make other people so happy.

"Now, on to number two match," said Fiona.

• • 🐙 • •

"I'm scared," Harold said.

"Don't be silly." Fiona grabbed a towel from the bathroom. She draped it over his shoulders.

"What's that?"

"What?" said Fiona.

"That!" Harold pointed to the bottle in Fiona's hand.

"Hair goop."

"Oh, Boise Idaho."

"You want to be like Milo, right?" Fiona poured the goop in her hands. She rubbed them together and wiped them on Harold's head.

"Burrito supreme," said Harold, "it feels cold."

Fiona's hands gathered and twisted Harold's hair into spiky points. But the points didn't stay spiky. Or pointy. "Hmmm."

"What's the matter?" asked Harold. "Can I see?"

"Not yet." Fiona squeezed. "How do you think he gets it to stand up like that?"

"Oh, Boise Idaho."

"Some big sister," said Max, appearing in the doorway. "Hey, why are you doing that to his hair?"

"Never mind," said Fiona. "Where's Cleo?"

"She went home," said Max. "Will you play with me now?" Max jumped up and down and pulled his cape over his head like a hood.

"I'm busy," said Fiona.

"I'll play," said Harold.

Max looked Harold over. "Um, that's okay," he said. And he was gone.

Fiona tapped her foot and patted Harold's goopy head while she thought. "Just a second." She opened her desk drawer and rooted around. "Don't move."

"What are you doing?" asked Harold.

"It's in here somewhere," said Fiona. She tossed out her box of broken crayons, dried-up markers, glitter pens, and bag of felt scraps. "Found it!" She

emptied the bottle onto Harold's head. Then she

pinched and pulled at his hair.

"Fiona?"

"What?"

"I smell glue."

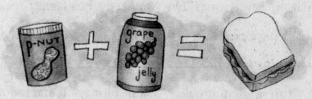

iona's dad looked like he had just eaten ten corned beef sandwiches. It wasn't pretty. "What were you thinking?" he asked. Fiona had heard this question lots of times before. And there was no good answer.

Fiona swiveled on Turner and thought about what she was thinking. Which was a not-so-easy thing to do. Especially when all of the green blobs on Dad's computer screen looked just like a bunny rabbit with giant fangs.

Dad leaned on his desk at WORD news station and waited.

"Harold wanted to be popular. That was his match," said Fiona. "Do you have a headache?"

"A big one," said Dad. "What do you mean that it was his match?"

"I'm a matchmaker," said Fiona. "I started a club at school and Harold wanted to be like Milo Bridgewater."

"And you thought glue in his hair was the way to go?"

Fiona said, "How else do you get hair to stand up?"

Dad's eyes got a little bulgy. But he didn't say anything, which made Fiona think he didn't know so much about hair. "Harold's grandmother said she doesn't want you playing with him anymore."

"It's not all my fault that his grandma cut it out," said Fiona. "I told Harold not to let his grandma see it."

. . ᚥ . .

Dad pulled at his eyebrow and sighed.

Fiona watched the bunny rabbit with fangs turn into a T. rex. Then she spun around on Turner, hugging her knees to her chest.

"Milo Bridgewater?" said Dad, clicking his mouse and looking at his computer screen.

"Milo Bridgewater," she repeated as if his name tasted like cauliflower.

"I think he's the boy who sent an e-mail to the station about starting a meteorology club at your school," he said. "He wants to learn more about the equipment we use here to produce some kind of news program."

Fiona stopped spinning. "What did you tell him?"

"I told him that I think it's a great idea."

She buried her face between her knees and squeezed her eyes shut. She remembered a movie on TV where Superman spun the earth in the opposite direction to turn back time so he could save Lois Lane. And so as fast as she could, she spun Turner in the opposite direction. To save herself from Milo Bridgewater.

It was too bad she didn't have any super-powers.

Loretta Cormley and Max were playing a game of Fish on the living room floor when Fiona got home. "Give me all your kings," said Loretta.

"Where's Mrs. Miltenberger?" asked Fiona.

Loretta said, "Bingo."

"Go fish," said Max. "And I'm not talking to her." He jabbed his finger in Fiona's direction.

"He's not talking to you," Loretta told her.

"What did I do?"

Max turned away and Loretta shrugged.

Fiona huffed. Some matchmaker she had turned out to be. She perched herself on the arm of the couch and watched the game.

Loretta pulled her cell phone out of her jacket pocket and dialed. After a few moments with the phone to her ear, she sighed and then snapped it shut. "Do you guys want to go somewhere?"

The seats inside Loretta Cormley's car had gray tape on them, and a cardboard tree hanging from the mirror made it smell like cinnamon spice. Fiona and Max rode in the backseat, and Loretta told them to be on the lookout for a cute boy with beautiful eyes. It was getting dark outside, which made it hard for Fiona's eyeballs to see anything.

Loretta pulled in front of Ordinary Java and parked. "Want some java?" she asked, as she turned off the car and opened the door.

Java was coffee, Loretta explained. Which was very disappointing to Fiona because "java" sounded like "lava" but had nothing at all to do with a volcano. "I had a sip of coffee once," Fiona told her, "but I spit it out because it tasted like earwax."

They went inside. "Why is it so dark in here?"

Fiona asked. Ordinary Java had red walls with paintings on them, couches and coffee tables, rugs with fringes, and lamps with shades sort of like the ones in the Finkelstein's living room. Teenagers were everywhere, and Fiona hoped that one day she would learn to like the taste of earwax so she could hang out at this place.

"Wait here," said Loretta.

Fiona watched as Loretta walked around and talked to other cool teenagers. Max pressed his face against the glass at the dessert counter.

Loretta returned. "He's not here," she said. "Ready to go?"

"Who's not here?" asked Fiona.

"Jeremy," said Loretta.

Max bent the tentacles on his Squidman action figure. "Who is Jeremy?"

"That's what I'm trying to figure out," said Loretta. "Who is the real Jeremy?"

Max and Fiona looked at each other. Fiona

shrugged. Teenagers were so mysterious.

When they were back in the car, Loretta sighed. "He could learn a few things from Noah Wycroft. Why is it that boys on TV are so much more mature?"

"I know Noah Wycroft," said Fiona. "I mean, I've never met him or anything. But I know who he is." He was a character on her mom's TV show, *Heartaches and Diamonds*.

"Yeah. I've written him, like, a ton of times. I mean, I've written Oliver Piff, the actor who plays Noah. But he's never written me back. Do you watch that show?"

"Sometimes," said Fiona. "My mom plays Scarlet von Tussle."

"No way!" said Loretta. "You're so lucky!"

Most people said the same thing about Fiona's mom being an actress on TV. But Fiona couldn't always share their excitement.

"I thought Jeremy and I would be such a good

match," said Loretta. "We're in all the same clubs. And he was even talking about giving up eating meat. I thought he liked me."

Max leaned his head against the car window and began to snore. "Too bad Noah's a made-up person," said Fiona.

"Yeah, too bad."

"I wish I could help," said Fiona. "But my match-making days are over." It was another declaration.

"How come?"

Fiona yawned. "I'm no good at it." What if she wasn't extraordinary at anything? What if she was going to be ordinary for the rest of her life?

Then Loretta suddenly said, "There he is!" She pulled the car up to a basketball court across from Baker's Square. "I'll be right back."

Fiona watched from the window as Loretta marched right into the middle of the basketball game. Loretta waved her arms in the air at this Jeremy boy while the other basketballers watched.

And that's when Fiona saw Milo. He had his hands stuffed in his jeans pockets, and he was staring at Loretta and this boy.

Fiona had something she wanted to say to Milo. And she didn't want to wait until school to do it. She closed the car door gently so she wouldn't wake up Max, and she headed straight for Milo. His eyes were on Loretta and the boy, so he didn't see her until she was right in front of him. "Milo Bridgewater," she said. He jumped back a little. "I think you should give up your meteorology club," said Fiona.

Milo must have been shocked by her declaration because he didn't say anything.

"Don't you have anything to say?" asked Fiona.

"You know her?" he asked, pointing to Loretta.

He sure was good at changing the subject. "Loretta's my watcher. Anyway," she said, "like I was saying, if you do give up your meteorology club, then I'll give up my S.N.O.W.-slash-A.W.S.O.M.M. club. Deal?"

For a gazillion years he didn't say anything. And the only thing Fiona could think of to do next was shake his hand. But Fiona wasn't an experienced hand shaker, and at the last minute, she couldn't remember which hand you were supposed to shake with. So, she reached out with both of her hands toward Milo, grabbing his shoulders. Then she gave them a shake.

Milo stepped backward. "No way," he said as he knocked into his bike.

By the look on his face, Fiona figured she must have looked real scary. Like a brain-eating zombie from one of those movies she was not allowed to watch but sometimes did anyway.

Or worse, like she was trying to give him a hug. Boy, oh, boy, she hoped Milo didn't think she was trying to hug him.

As Milo got on his bike and pedaled down Augusta Street, Fiona didn't know if he was saying "no way" to giving up his club or to a hug that she wasn't trying to give him anyway. She didn't want him to get the wrong idea, so she yelled after him, "It's okay, Milo, I don't *like*-like you!"

iona pressed her forehead into the frosted window of the school bus. OUTER SPACEY she wrote with her finger. Then she leaned forward and wrote SORRY CLEO and drew an unhappy face on the window of the seat in front of her.

Cleo peered over the seat.

"I'm sorry I matched you up with Max," said Fiona.

Cleo shrugged. "Are all little brothers like that?"

"I'm pretty sure."

Cleo made a sour face. "I don't think I'm ready for a little brother or sister."

"They aren't the worst thing," said Fiona. "You get used to them. Sort of."

When Fiona got to her classroom, she started on a new Thinking Pencil, an orange one. She kept her eye on the door for Harold.

Just when she began to think he wasn't coming to school today, there he was. Whatever Fiona imagined his hair to look like, this was gobs worse. Harold was wearing a hat, an old lady's straw hat with a ribbon around it. Fiona and Cleo looked at each other and then back at Harold.

Kids started laughing as soon as they saw him, until Mr. Bland gave them one of his scary teacher looks. Fiona followed that up with a Doom Scowl, with maximum doom.

"Harold," Mr. Bland said. "Your grandmother called this morning and said you would have a note for me?"

Harold reached into his pocket and handed Mr. Bland a folded paper. As Mr. Bland read the note to himself, Harold looked around the room. When his eyes stopped on hers, Fiona smiled. But Harold just pushed his hat down over his eyes.

"Just curious," Mr. Bland said. "A regular knit hat wouldn't work?"

Harold shook his head. "Too scratchy."

"Of course."

When Harold got to his desk, Fiona whispered, "Is it really that bad?"

"Would I be wearing this if it wasn't?" said Harold.

Good point.

"Mr. Bland," said Leila Rad, "why does he get to wear that, but you wouldn't let me wear my beret last month?"

"This is a special circumstance," explained Mr. Bland.

"What kind of—" said Leila Rad.

"If Harold wants to tell you what happened, he can do that on his own time," said Mr. Bland. "But I'm done discussing it. Take out your history books and let's get going."

"Is that from your makeover?" Cleo whispered, pointing to Harold.

Fiona nodded.

Cleo shook her head. "And I thought *I* had it bad."

Just then Fiona felt something hit her in the side of the head. "Ooof!" It landed on her desk, a paper football with her name in scribbled letters.

She opened it slowly and read.

Florida,
Meet me at recess by the seesaws.
Minnesota

Fiona quickly looked over at Milo, but he was busy writing something in a notebook. What did he want? She had never gotten hit in the head with a note from a boy before. She hoped he had heard her say that she didn't *like*-like him.

Finally, when recess came, Fiona left Cleo by the jungle gym and headed for the seesaws. "Any sign of trouble," said Cleo, making fists, "and I'll take care of him."

Milo waited with arms folded across his chest. Fiona crossed her own arms and said, "I wasn't trying to hug you at the basketball court."

"I know," he said.

"Okay, good," said Fiona. "I just wanted to make sure."

"Fine."

"Fine." Fiona tapped her foot. "What do you want?"

Milo uncrossed his arms and shoved his hands

into his pockets. "You can be president of my meteorology club if you want."

"Whaagh?" This was the last thing that Fiona expected to hear. "Why would you go and say a thing like that?"

"I need your help," he said.

This boy was a surprise box. "*My* help?"

"I know you have this matchmaking club," said Milo. "But I need your help with match*breaking*."

"Match*breaking*?"

"Yeah," said Milo. "We need to break up my brother and his girlfriend. She's your babysitter."

"Watcher," said Fiona. "I don't have a babysitter. I'm nine." Then what he was saying sunk in. "Wait a second, you mean Loretta Gormley?" Milo nodded. "And your brother is named Jeremy?" Milo nodded again.

"But why?"

"Because."

"I'm no breaker-upper," said Fiona. "You're barking at the wrong door."

"It can't be that hard," he said. "It's just like matchmaking but in reverse."

"I don't know how to matchmake," said Fiona. "Besides, even if I did, I wouldn't help you. I like Loretta. And she *like*-likes your brother. So."

"But I've been thinking about this, and Loretta and my brother are a terrible match. You should see Jeremy. He's always in a bad mood and doesn't want to hang out with me like he used to."

Fiona shook her head.

"Look," said Milo. "If you help me with this, I'll . . . I'll join your matchmaking club and tell everybody how awesome it is. Even though it's not." He grinned.

Fiona rolled her eyes at that. "Nope."

"Why not?"

"I told you a gazillion times already. I stink at matchmaking. Just ask Harold."

"Huh?"

"Harold wanted to be popular, that was his match. So I gave him a makeover. And now he looks like his granny."

Milo looked around the playground. "Harold wanted to be popular?"

"Yep."

Milo grinned so wide Fiona could see teeth. "Then you *can* matchmake. Look." Milo pointed past the swings.

Fiona looked across the kickball field and could not believe what she saw. Harold, with his hat off and patches of bald spots all over his head, was surrounded by gobs of kids. At first she thought that they must be trying to beat him up. But then, after she looked closer, she saw that he was smiling and laughing. "Oh, Boise Idaho," said Fiona. "How did that happen?

"Look, you have to," Milo said. "I've never seen Jeremy so . . ." He stuck out his tongue and crossed

his eyes. "Like that. I bet Loretta is the same way."

"I've never seen Loretta look like *that* before." Still, Fiona had to admit, Loretta didn't seem very happy. She was always looking at her cell phone and wondering why Jeremy hasn't called. "Maybe," she said.

"Jeremy and Loretta are like . . . like . . . I don't know what they're like."

"Ice cream and soy sauce?" suggested Fiona.

"Huh?"

"Lemon juice and milk? Cotton candy and ketchup?" She was on a roll. "Cauliflower and everything?

"You're weird."

Fiona shrugged.

"Deal?" Milo stuck out his hand. "But no hugs."

Fiona rolled her eyes and shook his hand. "We need a name."

"I know, I've already got one," he said. "The Duo Of Ordinary Matchbreakers."

Fiona repeated the name to herself and then said, "D.O.O.M.?"

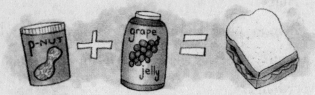

Chapter 12

Fiona waited for Milo at Button's Family Restaurant. Cleo's mom and dad owned the place, and sometimes Fiona helped Cleo fill the salt and pepper shakers and sugar jars after school. She ordered a strawberry milkshake extra thick and sat in a booth.

"Why do you want to be president of Milo's club when you could be president of your own club?" asked Cleo, sliding in beside her.

Fiona stirred her shake with her straw. "Because a president of a club with lots of people in it is a gazillion times better than a president of a club with zero people."

"I'm not a zero people," said Cleo, cracking her knuckles.

"I know that."

"Then why didn't you start a meteorology club when Principal Sterling asked you to?" said Cleo. "You could have had lots of people in it."

"I don't think so."

"What do you mean?" said Cleo. "Look at all the people in Milo's club!" She started to name them all.

"I'm not a Milo." Fiona turned her shake upside down and not a drop spilled.

"No, you're a Fiona." Cleo shook her head. "I have to fill the salt and pepper shakers."

Fiona worked on her milkshake and had three brain freezes before Milo got there. "Here," said Milo, holding out a plastic bubble like the kind you get in the prize machine at Foodland. "If we're a duo of D.O.O.M., I thought we'd need these."

Fiona popped open the bubble and held up the skull-and-crossbones ring that was inside.

"Cool, huh?" said Milo, holding up his hand and showing off the same ring on his finger. "Like the Dynamic Duo, except we're the Duo of D.O.O.M."

Fiona shook her head and put it on. "Boys are so weird," she said. "No wonder matchmaking is impossible."

Milo made a face and then said, "What's the plan?"

"I don't know," said Fiona. "I told you, I've never matchbreaked before. Or is it matchbroke?"

"Just do the opposite of what you did for matchmaking," said Milo. "Like what you did for Harold."

"I put glue and goop in his hair."

"Oh." Milo played with his skull ring. "I don't think that would work."

"No."

For a long time nobody said anything. Fiona got out her Thinking Pencil.

"Is there somebody we could ask for help?" said Milo.

"Like who? Somebody who has been broken up before?" she said.

"Exactly!" said Milo. "Now we're thinking!"

"Who in the world would that be?"

"Well, it would have to be a grown-up," said Milo.

"Then you'll have to do the asking," said Fiona. "I made a declaration of independence that I'm not asking grown-ups for advice on account of the fact that their advice stinks. Besides, I don't know anybody who's been broken up."

Milo tapped his fingers on the table while Fiona started chewing on her Thinking Pencil. "What about your mom?" asked Milo. "Doesn't she live in California?"

"How did you know that?"

"Harold told me," said Milo.

"I don't know what Harold told you, but my mom and dad aren't broken up," said Fiona. "My mom's a TV actress, and California is just where she works. That's all."

"I just meant that a TV actress would know about breakups."

"Oh. Maybe." The character her mom played, Scarlet von Tussle, had been married four or five times already. So she did know at least something about breaking up. "But what about my declaration of independence declaration?"

"What if the advice she gives you is for me, not for you?" said Milo. "Then you could still keep your declaration."

"Okay, fine." Fiona pulled her cell phone from her backpack and called California.

"You caught me on the way home from rehearsal," said Mom. "What's up?"

"I was wondering," said Fiona, "how do you break up people?"

"What? I'm having a hard time hearing you." Fiona heard a loud whirring of machines in the background. "There's a lot of construction on the highway. You want to know how to do what?"

"Break up people," said Fiona, louder.

"Oh, you want to break up people?"

"Right," said Fiona.

"What's this about? Who do you want to break up?"

"Loretta and Jeremy," said Fiona. "You don't know them."

"Okay, excellent. In that case, I would say . . . Hey, watch it! Sorry, Fiona, are you still there?"

"Yep."

"The drivers out here are the worst. Everybody's in a hurry. Can't be late. Anyway, what was I saying? Oh, right, the best way to break up a couple is to make one of them think the other one likes somebody else."

"That works?" asked Fiona.

"Like a charm. As a matter of fact, that's just what happened with Noah Wycroft and Annabelle McGibbons on yesterday's episode. . . ."

Fiona stopped listening at that point, because an idea landed right in her lap. She hung up the phone and took a piece of paper out of her backpack. "We need to write a letter from Oliver Piff to Loretta."

"Who's Oliver Piff?"

"The guy who plays Noah Wycroft on TV," explained Fiona.

"Who's Noah Wycroft?" Milo said.

"The guy Loretta likes."

"She does? Since when?"

"Since I don't know," said Fiona. "She talks about him sometimes."

"When does she talk about him?" asked Milo, eyes narrow.

"Milo," Fiona said, waving her hand in front of his face, "that's not important." She held up the piece of paper. "The letter, remember?"

Milo nodded. "What kind of letter are we going to write?"

"An L-O-V-E letter," said Fiona.

"No, a D.O.O.M. letter," he said, smiling.

• Chapter 13 •

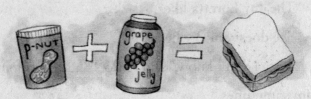

aybe it was the two extra thick strawberry milkshakes, but after she got home Fiona felt heavy. And lost. Like the time she wandered around forever in the corn maze at Crumland Farm and had to throw her shoe up in the air to let them know she needed to be rescued. Every turn she made was a wrong one, getting her farther away from where she wanted to be.

But where was that exactly? And if being president didn't get you there, then what in the world did? When would she get to be extra-ordinary?

Fiona plopped on the couch and pulled off her shoes. Questions filled her brain like buttons in a jar. The biggest of them all was sitting right on top: Why *didn't* she start a meteorology club back when Principal Sterling asked her to? She turned that button over and over again in her head.

She tossed her shoe into the air and caught it. The answer came to her then like it had been there all the time: "I don't want to be club president," she said out loud. And as soon as she said it, things seemed to be a little less outer spacey.

"What are you doing?" asked Max.

"I'm rescuing myself." She threw her shoe again.

Max took off his flipper and tossed it into the air. It landed behind him.

"Here, catch," she said, throwing his flipper like a Frisbee across the room. Max dove for it and almost caught it before tripping on the rug. "You okay?"

He grabbed the flipper and threw it back to her, laughing.

She caught it and hugged it to her chest.

"Are you going to give me away to Cleo anymore?" he asked.

"No," Fiona said. "I guess you're stuck with me."

"Good. Like lima beans and corn?" said Max.

"Like lima beans and corn," she said, smiling. And then she remembered. "Loretta!"

Fiona waited for Milo in front of school the next morning. As soon as he rode up on his bike, she bolted at him, almost knocking him down. "Where's the letter?"

"Hey there, President," he said.

"The letter!" she said. "You have to give me Loretta's letter!"

"I can't."

"Yes, you can," she said. "I changed my mind. I don't want to be a breaker-upper."

"Too late," he said, smiling. "Mission accomplished."

"What does that mean?" asked Fiona.

"I rode by Loretta's house on the way to school and put the letter in her mailbox."

"You did what? How did you even know how to get to her house?" Fiona scratched her head.

"I got directions on the Internet," he said.

"Ahhh!" Fiona rubbed her eyes.

"What's wrong?" he said. "I typed it up on the computer like you told me and then I delivered it. Hey, where's your D.O.O.M. ring?"

"Here," said Fiona. She pulled the plastic ring out of her pocket and handed it to him. "I quit."

• Chapter 14 •

ad!" Fiona yelled when she got home.

"In the study!" he called back.

She ran down the hall and poked her head in the door. "Do you have Loretta's phone number?"

"Loretta?" Dad squinted his eyes like he had to think about that one. Sometimes he liked to pretend he didn't know what Fiona was talking about. Which Fiona usually thought was a fun game to play, but not when she was trying to stop a matchbreak.

"Come on, Dad!" said Fiona. "You know, Loretta. My watcher."

"Should be on the phone list on the refrigerator," he said.

"Thanks." She started back down the hall.

"Hey, I want to talk to you," he said.

"Right now?" she said from the hallway.

"Suits me."

Fiona stuck her head back inside the door. "Yeah, Dad?" She tapped her toe impatiently.

"Have a seat," he said.

"But . . ."

"It will only take a minute," he said. "I've hardly seen you lately, Dancing Bean."

Fiona sat in the chair across from his desk and waited. She couldn't tell if she was in trouble or not. Dad was good at springing trouble on you.

"Remember when I said that a student, Milo something or other, wanted to start a news program at your school?"

"Milo Bridgewater," said Fiona. "Also known as electrician, president, and D.O.O.M breaker-upper."

"Wow, that's quite a résumé," he said. "Anyway, we've been talking to Principal Sterling, and she thinks it's a great idea for WORD to be a partner."

"That's great," said Fiona, getting up. "Sounds really fun."

"Sit, sit," he said. "That's not all."

Fiona sat in her chair, but she couldn't stop her feet from moving.

Dad leaned forward at his desk. "This Milo fellow seems to be really interested in meteorology, and Principal Sterling wants Milo to be involved in producing that part of the news program."

"Oh," said Fiona.

"Well, since you are the snow angel and give weather reports for the station," said Dad, "I just wanted to see how you feel about that."

Fiona thought about what he was saying. Since Milo was going to still be president of the meteorology club, it made sense that he was part of the news program. She looked at her feet. They didn't feel stepped on. "I'm fine about it."

"Really? You're sure?"

"Could I still do my snow angel weather reports at WORD if I wanted to?" she asked.

"Of course," he said. "This would only be for your school news program."

Fiona nodded. "Then, okay. Yep. Sounds fine and dandy. Can I go now?"

"I'll take a kiss first," said Dad. "And then you can go. Unless you want to tell me more about this matchmaking club of yours and Harold Chutney's hair."

"No, thanks," she said, and then she kissed his cheek and ran to the kitchen.

She dialed Loretta's number and left the

following message: "Loretta Gormley, we have a watcher emergency. Please report to the Finkelstein's house as soon as you get this message. And do not open your mail. I repeat, do not open your mail. This is not a test."

• Chapter 15 •

From the front window, Fiona watched and waited for Loretta.

"Expecting company?" asked Mrs. Miltenberger.

Fiona kept her eyes out the window. "Yep."

"Anybody I know?"

"Yep."

"Well, don't leave me in suspense," said Mrs. Miltenberger.

Fiona's brain was set on how she was going to get that letter before Loretta read it. "Yep."

"Fiona Finkelstein," said Mrs. Miltenberger, "are you listening to a word I'm saying?"

"Yep."

Mrs. Miltenberger cleared her throat. "So, then, you're going to clean your closet right after you scrub the inside of the microwave?"

"Yep . . . huh?" said Fiona. "Wait a second."

"Gotcha." Mrs. Miltenberger laughed. "So, you've got a boyfriend coming over?"

"Gross nuggets, I don't have a boyfriend," said Fiona. "Loretta is coming over." Then she saw her car coming down the street. "She's here!" Fiona ran out the front door to meet her.

"I got your message," said Loretta, getting out of her car. "What's the watcher emergency?"

Fiona looked in the window of Loretta's car for the letter. "Um, did you get your mail today?"

"As a matter of fact, I did. Why?"

Fiona stomped her foot nervously. "Did you read it?"

"As a matter of fact, I did."

"Oh." A corned beef feeling came over Fiona.

"Okay if I come in?" asked Loretta. "The watcher emergency, you know."

"Oh, right," said Fiona. "Okay."

"Loretta, what a nice surprise," said Mrs. Miltenberger, greeting her at the door. "Come on in."

"So," said Fiona. "Did you get anything interesting in the mail today?"

Loretta reached into her corduroy purse and pulled out a piece of paper. Then she did something Fiona didn't expect. She covered her face with her hands and started making these wheezy hiccupping sounds.

"What's the matter?" asked Fiona. She thought she'd be happy to get a letter from Oliver Piff. But then again, maybe she was sad because she would have to break up with Jeremy Bridgewater. Who knew? The mystery of teenagers.

Loretta held out the letter, and that's when
Fiona could tell she was laughing. "What's so
funny?"

"Read it," said Loretta.

Fiona and Mrs. Miltenberger read it at the
same time.

My favorite and biggest fan
Loretia Gormley,

 I am sorr y I did not write you
a leter before this one. I am very busy
on *Heartaches and Diamonds* where I am
character that's in all sorts of scenes
with other people. You'd think I'd be
matched up with someone else, because I
am very cute and have beautiful eyes,
but I am not. When I read your letters,
it makes me think YOU are my match,
Loretia Gormley.

 Maybe we can meat someday even
though you live in Maryland and I live in
Californa. If you *like*-like somebody now,
please stop. I can't bare to think about
you like-liking somebody else. Check
the box below and sign your name if
you agree.

❑ Okay, I will stop like-liking Jeremy.

Sign here: _____

Your Match 4ever,

Oliver Piff (that's Noah Wycroft on TV)

Before Fiona could get to the end, Mrs. Miltenberger was laughing so hard she had to sit down.

"I don't get it," said Fiona. She looked at the letter again and saw a couple of misspellings and wrong words, but nothing that made her laugh. "What's so funny?"

"It's Lor-ee-sha," said Loretta, hardly able to talk. "Not Loretta."

Oh. So, Milo wasn't the best typer and she wasn't the best speller. Still, it wasn't *that* funny.

"Jeremy's younger brother wrote this to try to break us up," said Loretta. "Fiona, was this your watcher emergency?"

Fiona nodded. "Wait a second, how do you know that Milo wrote it?"

"My admirer," said Loretta, grinning. "When I called Jeremy and told him about the letter, he had a talk with his brother. He was really very sweet about it."

"Sweet about what?" asked Fiona. She was more than confused. She was lost.

"About me," said Loretta, putting her hand over her heart. "Milo has a crush on me."

"Let me get this straight," said Fiona, shaking her head clear. "Milo has liked you all this time. I mean, he *like*-likes you, and that's why he wanted you to break up? Not because you and Jeremy are a terrible match and you both are . . ." She stuck out her tongue and crossed her eyes. "Like that?"

"What? I don't know about that last part, but yep, that's pretty much right," said Loretta. She picked up the letter again and read, "'Maybe we can m-e-a-t someday.'" That got Mrs. Miltenberger's giggles going again.

Fiona shook her head. She could not believe Milo had tricked her. She had even worn that stupid skull ring!

Loretta cleared her throat. "He also said he had a little help with the letter."

Fiona felt her face go Valentine's Day red.

"So, you and Jeremy are—" asked Fiona.

"Broken up," said Loretta.

"Oh!" said Fiona. Now she had to sit down.

"We aren't broken up because of this letter," said Loretta, laughing even more. "I decided that, like, we just weren't a good match after all."

"Whew." Fiona put her head down on the table. "All this matchmaking and matchbreaking makes me tired. I'm done."

"That's too bad," says Mrs. Miltenberger. "I was thinking about giving you a chance to make a match for me. You can't do worse than the Bingo Broads."

"Sorry, I'm out of business."

"Well, what's your next club going to be?" asked Mrs. Miltenberger.

Fiona shrugged. "I don't think I'm extraordinary enough at anything to have a club."

"What?" said Loretta.

"Not extraordinary?" said Mrs. Miltenberger, knocking on the table. "Who says?"

"Me," said Fiona. "Fiona says."

"Phoozywhattle," said Mrs. Miltenberger. "What do you think 'extraordinary' means?"

"It means the opposite of ordinary," said Fiona. "Special."

"'Extraordinary' can also mean strange and unusual," said Loretta, raising her eyebrows at Fiona. "Mysterious."

"Mysterious?"

Loretta nodded.

"Mysterious," Fiona repeated, smiling. Just like a teenager.

"One of a kind," said Mrs. Miltenberger. "There

is only one Fiona Elise Finkelstein. Ballet dancer, snow angel, matchmaker."

"Match*breaker*," added Loretta.

"And if that's not extraordinary," said Mrs. Miltenberger, "then I don't know what is."

"One of a kind, huh?" said Fiona, thinking it over. "Kind of like snowflakes."

"Snowflakes?" said Loretta.

"No two are alike." Now *that's* extraordinary. But Fiona never thought about herself that way before. "There *is* only one me. And I am pretty good at being her."

"The best," said Mrs. Miltenberger.

Fiona smiled. "That's flat-out something."

· Epilogue ·

Fiona chomped on her Thinking Pencil. She eyed the clock in Mr. Bland's classroom and then eyed Mr. Bland. It was the last day of the month, which meant it was Milo Bridgewater's last day as electrician. Which meant that tomorrow—fingers crossed—could be her first. She had already asked Mr. Bland twice when he was going to draw names for classroom jobs. "I'll let you know when I decide," he had said.

But Fiona couldn't wait any longer. The day was almost over. She raised her hand again. When

Mr. Bland looked the other way, she shook her hand at him. First, she shook it slowly, like a shivering apple. Then, when he still didn't call on her, she shook it wildly, like a wet dog. "If you ask me one more time about classroom jobs, Fiona Finkelstein," Mr. Bland said in a calm voice that had splinters in it, "I'm going to remove your name from the bucket."

Some of the splinters stuck. She dropped her hand and gave him a Doom Scowl, an invisible one so that he couldn't see, with extra Doom. Fiona must have looked like she was about to say something else just then, because Cleo whispered her name and then moved her fingers across her lips like a zipper.

Fiona nodded. She locked her mouth with her fingers and threw the key over her shoulder. Because she knew that when it came to her mouth, a zipper wasn't strong enough to do the trick. Her mouth had made a declaration of independence from her a long time ago.

"Before you pack up to go home," said Mr. Bland, "remember that tomorrow we're going to have our first rehearsal for Ordinary Elementary News."

"O.E.N.?" Fiona whispered to Milo. "We need a better name."

"I know it," he said.

After the Loretta L-O-V-E Letter Incident, Fiona and Milo declared world peace. Fiona gave up on starting any new school clubs, *for now*. (Especially after Mr. Bland declared that from now on, all new ideas for school clubs had to be approved by him.) Milo gave up on Loretta on account of the fact that teenagers were too mysterious. And they both gave up on D.O.O.M.

Like soy sauce and ice cream, there were just some things that didn't go together.

"Milo," said Mr. Bland, "do you have some announcements you want to make?"

Milo stood at his desk gripping a clipboard and a pencil. "Everybody knows what they are supposed to do for tomorrow?"

Fiona stared at the bucket marked ELECTRICIAN underneath the job board. If only she had X-ray eyes so she could see the paper with her name on it. And if only she could talk to trees, she thought, then she could talk to paper—since paper is made from trees. She could sing a lullaby to that piece of paper with her name on it and tell it to latch on to Mr. Bland's fingers so that when he reached into the bucket, she would finally get to be . . .

"Fiona?"

"Huh?" she said, turning to the front of the room.

"Your interview with Principal Sterling," said Milo. "Do you have the questions that you're going to ask?"

Fiona shook her head.

"You don't?"

"I changed my mind," she said. "I had a big idea this morning when I checked my lunch box and saw that Mrs. Miltenberger had packed me a peanut butter and strawberry jelly sandwich."

"Fiona," said Mr. Bland, rubbing his head, "we only have a few minutes before the bell."

Fiona sped up her words. "So instead of interviewing Principal Sterling, I was thinking about a news report on the history of food couples."

"Food what?" said Milo.

"You know," she said, "food couples. Partners. Buddies. Like macaroni and cheese, spaghetti and meatballs."

"Pork and beans," said Harold.

"Good one," said Fiona, writing that down. "And how they got to be matched up."

"What about Principal Sterling?" asked Milo.

"I'll do it," said Cleo. "I'll interview her. I'd rather do that than operate the camera."

Milo shrugged and then nodded. "Leila, do you want to be the cameraman?"

"Camera*girl*," Leila corrected. "Okay."

"All right, Florida."

"Thanks, Minnesota," Fiona said.

Milo grinned. "Harold, you're the stage manager. You got your checklist?"

Harold wiped his finger on his pants and then gave the a-ok sign. "You betcha."

While Milo went on to check in with others about their jobs, Fiona whispered to Harold, "Want to come over after school and help me find more food matchups for my report?"

"Can't," said Harold. "Leila invited me over to her house to help her rearrange her stuffed animal collection. Sorry."

"That's okay." The new, popular Harold was something she still had to get used to.

When Milo finished, Fiona looked quickly at the clock and then at Mr. Bland. He was headed in the direction of the Job Center, and by the time he reached it, Fiona had all of her fingers crossed.

Mr. Bland reached into the first bucket and said something, but Fiona's heart was beating so loud in her ears, she couldn't tell what.

He reached into the second, and then the third. Fiona wanted to stick her fingers in her ears to quiet her heart, but she didn't dare uncross them.

Finally, he got to the electrician bucket. Fiona repeated her name, at first to herself, and then out loud and over top of her thumping heart. Mr. Bland took a gazillion years to unfold the piece of paper and she tried really hard not to leap out of her chair.

Then, finally, Mr. Bland looked right at Fiona. Her heart stopped making noise as he sighed. Then he shook his head and said, "Extraordinary."

And she knew it flat-out was.

Peanut butter was invented in 1890. A doctor in St. Louis, Missouri, made peanut paste for his patients with bad teeth who couldn't chew meat. Peanuts have a lot of protein in them, kind of like meat, but peanut butter is a lot easier to chew.

This doctor went up to George A. Bayle Jr., who owned a food company, and asked him to package his peanut paste. Mr. Bayle must have thought that was a pretty good idea, because he started selling peanut butter out of barrels for about six cents a pound. Can you imagine a whole barrel of peanut butter for just six pennies?

A few years later, another doctor named John Harvey Kellogg and his brother, W. K. Kellogg, got into the peanut butter business and got a patent in 1895 for the "Process of Preparing Nut Meal."

The first nut cookbook, called *The Complete Guide to Nut Cookery*, came out in 1899.

As for jelly . . . people have been eating jelly in America for hundreds of years. Colonials in the 1600s even used jelly as icing for cakes.

Nobody knows for sure when peanut butter and jelly first met. But some people think it happened during World War II. American soldiers ate a lot of peanut butter. And everybody knows that eating a lot of peanut butter can be a good thing if you like peanut butter. But after eating it for a gazillion days, it can get kind of old. So some people believe that American soldiers added jelly to their peanut butter to make it taste better. When the war ended and the soldiers came home, peanut butter and jelly was a big hit!

Now peanut butter and jelly sandwiches are in school cafeterias, on menus at restaurants, and in vending machines. There's even a peanut butter and jelly sandwich eating contest and a peanut-butter-and-jelly-of-the-month club!

Maybe it's because jelly is so sweet. Or maybe it's because peanut butter is just flat-out nutty. Who knows? But it's just like Mrs. Miltenberger says: They are a match made in sandwich heaven.

Here are some other peanut butter and jelly facts:

1: It takes about 540 peanuts to make one 12-ounce jar of peanut butter.

2: In September 2002, the world's largest peanut butter and jelly sandwich was made. It weighed 900 pounds and contained 350 pounds of peanut butter and 144 pounds of jelly.

3: Ninety-six percent of people spread the peanut butter on the bread first, and then the jelly.

4: The average child will eat about 1,500 peanut butter and jelly sandwiches before finishing high school.

5: The most common jelly used is grape (which is okay, but my favorite is crab apple). The second most common is strawberry.

There are lots of foods that you might think would be good together, but matchmaking is a lot harder than it looks. Believe me. Tune in next time to find out how spaghetti met meatballs. Well, I'll tell you this: They didn't meet at the movies, that's for sure.

• Acknowledgments •

Thanks go to my husband, Andy, first and forever foremost, for telling me that I don't stink (even when I do), for keeping me from burying my head in a pillow, and for always managing to make me laugh (even at myself). He is the mustard to my cheese sandwich on toast.

Thanks to my family, who puts the *extra* in extraordinary, for their love and encouragement. And for believing in me. And for not holding my teenage years against me. And for showing up at my book signings even when there aren't any cupcakes.

If I had the world's biggest peanut butter and jelly sandwich, I'd share it with all my friends as thanks, and would never declare independence from: Jess Leader, Ana Tavakoli, Annemarie O'Brien, Gene Brenek, Allyson Schrier, Amy Cabrera, Ellery Scott, Jennifer Tisch, Martha Sasser, Carol Lynch Williams, Debbie Gonzalez, Sarah Aronson, Tami Lewis Brown, and Theresa Fitzgerald.

For Sarah Davies of Greenhouse Literary Agency, a brightly colored bouquet of gratitude for saying the words all writers want to hear; and for my editor, Kate Angelella, a beautifully wrapped box of appreciation and admiration for her creative guidance, wit, and most of all, patience.